Contents

YOUNG MONSTERS

Michael Lawrence

Illustrated by Chris Mould

Barrington Stoke

For Linda and Ian

First published in 2003 in Great Britain by
Barrington Stoke Ltd
18 Walker Street, Edinburgh, EH3 7LP

www.barringtonstoke.co.uk

This edition first published 2014

A CIP catalogue record for this book is available
from the British Library upon request

ISBN: 978-1-78112-357-7

Printed in China by Leo

Chapter 1
Sent Away

Lon's father was forever calling him a "young monster". Lon didn't like this at all, but his father was a stern man. To tell the truth, Lon was a bit afraid of him. One day his father said –

"Lon, pack your bags. I'm sending you away."

"Away?" Lon gulped.

"To my old boarding school where they know just what to do with young monsters like you. I'll be popping in to see how you're getting on and, if I don't see improvements very soon, I shall be most unhappy."

So Lon was sent off in a pony and cart to his father's old boarding school. As they neared the gates, the pony reared up, almost tipping Lon and the driver out.

"Whoa, boy! Steady, steady!" the driver said. When the pony had settled down, the driver said to Lon, "This is as far as I'm taking you. Old Nell won't go through these gates."

Lon got down from the trap. The driver threw his bag out after him and drove away at speed. Lon stood at the gates of his new school, looking at the big sign beside them.

All of a sudden, a sharp voice said, "What is your business here?" The words came from the gates themselves.

Dr Ffelix Ffurter's School for Young Monsters

"I've been sent to study here," Lon replied.

"Another young monster!" the gates cried, and they swung open with a sound like sharp knives scraping across dinner plates. "Well, come in, come in. If you think I'm going to waste my day talking to you, you're wrong."

Lon walked inside. "Thanks very much," he said as the gates grumbled shut. He was a polite boy.

At the end of the weed-covered drive there stood a huge ramshackle house. When

Lon reached the front door, he seized the great iron knocker and banged it as hard as he dared. There was a pause. A really long pause, in which there was no sound of any kind. It was the kind of pause that gives a person ... how can I put it? The willies.

But then the door creaked open. Very, very slowly. Very, very creakily. Lon expected to find someone standing on the other side, but there was no one there. He went in, and found himself in a massive entrance hall full of cobwebs and shadows and rusty suits of armour.

"H-hello?" he said timidly as the door closed behind him. "Is there anybody here?"

He thought he heard a cackle of laughter. He looked about but could see no one. He decided he must have imagined it. But he did not imagine the large cat that ran at him and sank its sharp little teeth into his ankle.

"Eeeeeeyooooowaaaaaaaah!" said Lon (or something rather like it).

The echo of Lon's screech of pain bounced around from wall to wall and up and down the stairs for some time before it got fed up and fell to the floor in a sulk. Another silent willies-ish pause might have started up then if it had not been for the voice.

"You mustn't mind Tiddles," the voice said. "He loves boys' ankles, that's all."

It was a muffled voice, and it seemed to come from a large bowl of fruit on a tall trolley.

"Wh-where are you?" Lon said with a gulp.

"Somewhere between the grapes, the bananas and the rotten apples," the voice replied.

Lon removed some of the fruit and peered into the fruit bowl. There, right in the middle, was a human head.

And it was looking right at him.

Chapter 2
The Head

The head had the brightest blue eyes, the hairiest ginger eyebrows and the longest teeth that Lon had ever seen.

"Where's the rest of you?" Lon said, with some alarm.

"If you mean my body – well, it's a very sad tale. Would you like to hear it?"

"Not really," said Lon.

But the head told him anyway. "I was young and foolish and devil-may-care," he began. "I failed to listen to the advice of my monstrous elders and I took the bolt from my neck. When my head fell off, my body toppled over a cliff and was torn apart by eagles. Never ever remove your bolt, my boy. Look what can happen. Oh, but I see that you have no bolt. Well, we'll soon put that right."

"Who are you?" Lon asked.

"Oh, didn't I say? I'm Dr Ffelix Ffurter, Head of this fine establishment. And your name is ...?"

"Lon, sir. My father sent me here to study."

"Ah yes, our new Year 7. Get the rest of this fruit off me, there's a good lad."

"What's all this fruit doing round your head anyway?" Lon asked as he cleared the fruit away.

"I was hiding," the Head answered. "When I hide my head under a pile of fruit, not only can I keep an eye on the general comings and goings, but the vitamin C is good for my chin. Step this way, young fellow!"

The trolley whizzed round and rattled away, with the Head bobbing around on top of it. Lon followed. They came to a large door.

"Open!" the Head commanded.

The door flew back angrily, as if it would prefer to stay shut, or write a poem, or do something else entirely. The trolley shot inside and wheeled itself behind a big leather-topped desk. The Head peered across the desk at Lon.

"I see very little of the monster in you, boy," he said. "But your father wouldn't have sent you here if he didn't think there was *something* monstrous about you."

"No one thought I was very monstrous at my last school," Lon informed him. "In fact, I was quite popular there."

"What sort of school was it?" the Head asked.

"Oh, just an ordinary one. Very different from here."

As he said this, Lon swept his arm around the room. Sadly, the Head's study was very cluttered and Lon's sweeping arm sent a vase of dead flowers flying. The vase struck a large mirror, and the mirror shattered and fell to the floor in pieces. One of the pieces just missed Tiddles the cat, who had followed them, hoping for a nip at Lon's other ankle.

"A broken mirror," Dr Ffurter said cheerfully. "Another seven years' bad luck! Hmm, perhaps you're more of a monster than you look. You work hard, my boy, and in a year or two you might be ready to sit your GCME exam."

"My what?" Lon asked.

"The General Certificate of Monstrous Excellence. But first things first." He raised his voice. "Mrs Staines!" he called out.

There was a grumpy sigh from across the room, and the ghostly shape of a bad-tempered old woman leaned out of a panel in the wall.

"Is there no peace even in death?" the old woman snapped.

"Mrs Staines is my secretary," the Head told Lon. "Please be so good as to call a student," he said. "I have need of one."

Mrs Staines opened her mouth wide enough to swallow a football and screamed the most ear-splitting scream Lon had ever heard.

"Why is she screaming?" he cried.

"It's her way of calling boys," Dr Ffurter explained. "If the nearest boy doesn't hammer at my door within six seconds of that scream, he knows that Mrs Staines and a bunch of her horrible dead relatives will haunt him till the end of term."

Five and a half seconds after the scream had died away, there was a hammering at the door. "Come in!" the Head yelled.

The door flew open. A boy stood there. A scowling, green-faced boy with freckles and fangs. He had a hammer in his hand and a large bolt through his neck.

"Ah, Grout," said the Head. "I would like you to take our new student here to Matron to have his bolt fitted. When she's done with him, show him the way to Dorm 6, where a bed full of crushed cockroaches awaits him."

Grout replaced his hammer in the holster at his hip. "Right you are, sir," he said. Then he grabbed Lon's left ear and hauled it out of the room. You may not be surprised to learn that Lon followed quite closely behind.

Chapter 3
Grout

Now, Lon was a sweet-tempered lad, but
every so often he saw red. Seeing red, as you
probably know, means getting really annoyed.
Lon saw red as Grout dragged him along the
corridor by his left ear. (He would have been
just as annoyed if it had been his right ear,
but that's by the by.)

"Let me go!" he shouted, as he tried to
wiggle out of Grout's loutish grip.

"Not a chance," Grout said, with a grin so wide and sloppy that drool dribbled from the corners of his mouth. "I've decided I don't like you. You look much too normal to me."

The building was very old and gloomy, with cobwebs drooping from every corner and rats scampering at every turn. Grout stamped his foot down on the tail of one of the rats. The tail remained while the rat made its escape. Grout scooped up the tail and lowered it into his mouth like a strand of freshly cooked spaghetti. "Tasty," he said, slapping his lips.

When they reached Matron's room, Grout took out his hammer and banged on the door.

"Why don't you use your fist?" Lon said, twisting and turning in the bigger boy's grip.

Grout squeezed his ear even harder. "I save my fists for Year 7s," he said. "Besides, knocking on doors with your fists is what normal people do. I'm not normal. I'm a young monster."

"You don't say," said Lon.

The door opened into a small, cave-like room with one single high bed. On the bed sat a boy of about Lon's age. Like Grout, and every other boy they'd passed on the way, the boy had a large bolt through his neck. A plump woman with hairy warts on her face was looking through the boy's hair. Her nose was running, Lon noticed, though the rest of her stayed where it was.

"No," Matron said to the boy. "No lice. Not a single one. You'll really have to work harder to attract them, Omar. Down you get." The boy got down from the bed and Matron turned to Lon and Grout. "Now, what can I do for you two?"

Grout yanked Lon's ear towards the bed. "New kid for you, Matron. The Head sent him to –"

He was going to add "have his bolt fitted" – but just then Lon fell over Tiddles, the school cat, who had been trying to trip them up all the way from the Head's study. Lon's elbow flew back and struck Grout on the nose. Grout yelped. Blood spurted. Unlike most boys' blood, Grout's blood was green. It was also rather thick and sticky, like treacle (but probably not quite so nice on pancakes).

Lon tried to regain his balance. As he did so, his head came up under Grout's chin. Grout yelped again and hit the floor.

Lon hadn't meant these things to happen, of course, and he was sorry about them. "Sorry, sorry, sorry," he said, and he leaned down to help Grout up. But, to his horror, Grout's hand came away!

"Eergh!" Lon shouted, and he flung Grout's hand away from him. As the hand hurtled across the room, it became a fist and it struck the monster-fish tank under the window, smashing it to smithereens. Suddenly, the floor was awash with monster-fish, all bulgy

eyes and snappy little teeth. Tiddles ran for his life.

Meanwhile, Grout's hand seemed to be practising dance steps on the window ledge. It might have been quite happy to go on doing this for some time if it hadn't slipped. Over the ledge it went, down and down and down, until it came to rest in the jaws of Russ, the school dog. Russ had three heads and three sets of jaws. Each set of jaws gulped down a share of Grout's hand before you could say "Woof!"

"My favourite hand!" Grout wailed from the window.

"Don't worry," Matron said. "We'll dig up a new one for you."

"It won't be the same. I loved that hand. It was my grandpa's." Grout turned on Lon. "I'll get you for this, new kid!"

Lon tried to tell him that it had been an accident, but Grout refused to listen. He charged out of the room, swearing to make Lon pay for feeding his grandpa's hand to the school dog.

Chapter 4
Bolted

The boy without the head lice didn't believe it had been an accident either. He was impressed at the way Lon had dealt with Grout.

"Pleased to meet you," he said. "My name's Omar." He held out his hand. Lon eyed it with suspicion. "Don't worry," Omar said, "it won't come off. I'm not much of a monster. I'm a great let-down to my father," he added sadly.

"So am I to mine," said Lon.

"Now, why did the Head send you to me?" Matron asked Lon.

"Tell her it was for some ointment for his You-Know-What," Omar whispered to Lon.

"What's his You-Know-What?" Lon whispered back.

"I've no idea, but I've heard him mention it to Matron," Omar said. "And pull your collar up. Don't let her see your neck, whatever you do."

Lon pulled his collar up and turned to Matron. "The Head sent me to ask for some ointment for his You-Know-What."

"But I only gave him some on Friday," Matron said in surprise.

"He must have used it all up," Lon replied. He wished he knew what he was talking about.

Matron gave him a tub of ointment for the Head. The label said –

You-Know-What Ointment.
Keep out of reach of children
and DON'T SWALLOW!

Outside Matron's room, Lon turned to Omar. "Why did I have to lie to her?" he asked.

"I'm guessing that the Head sent you to have a bolt fitted," Omar said.

"Yes, he did. What is all this bolt stuff anyway?"

"At normal boarding schools, boys have to wear ties," Omar said. "At monster schools, they wear bolts through their necks instead.

Some kids come with their bolts already fitted, like Grout and his pals. They've had them since they were toddlers. The rest of us are bolted as soon as we arrive."

"Was your bolt fitted before or after you arrived?" Lon asked him.

"Neither," Omar said. "I fooled them. 'Once bolted, always bolted,' is what they say. I didn't want that. Do you want that?"

"Not really, now you mention it. But won't they notice if I don't have a bolt?"

"Not if you put this on," Omar said. He dipped into his pocket and pulled out a strap-on bolt. "It's my spare. You can have it. I'll write to my mum for another. She's not keen on bolting. It's my father who wants me to be a monster. He says it's the only way to get on in this world."

Omar strapped the bolt onto Lon's neck. It looked just like the real thing.

"That boy Grout was supposed to show me to Dorm 6," Lon said. "Any idea which way it is?"

"That's my dorm," Omar said with a smile. "Come on, I'll take you."

They set off through the long, gloomy corridors. "You've made an enemy of Grout," Omar said as they walked. "Rather you than me. Keep looking over your shoulder, that's my advice."

They climbed flight after flight of shadowy stairs. There were cobwebby shelves all the way up. On the shelves were skulls, jars of eyeballs like gobstoppers, and heaps of grinning teeth.

"I don't really know what monster schools are for," Lon said. "I should, because my father works for the Office of Monster Education. But he never talks about his work and I never ask. Isn't monstrous behaviour frowned upon in the outside world?"

"Dr Ffurter says that monsters play an important role in society," Omar told him. "He says that if humans aren't scared now and then by nightmare creatures, then they have trouble dealing with the boring slog of normal life."

There were several boys in Dorm 6 when they got there. All had bolts through their necks. Some also had huge eyes, or extra arms and legs, or were extremely hairy. Some growled, some looked scary, some looked plain silly. But a few of them seemed so normal that Lon was puzzled.

"They might look normal," Omar whispered, "but no one is sent here unless his

parents think he's a young monster. It doesn't always show, that's all."

"You look pretty normal too, come to that," Lon said.

Omar seemed rather upset by this. "I do try," he said. "Look." He pulled his worst monster face. Lon laughed. "No, no, no," said Omar. "It's meant to be scary, not funny!"

"I wasn't laughing," Lon said, hiding his grin. "I was shaking with terror."

This cheered Omar up. It was good to have a friend.

Chapter 5
The Task

Next morning, all students and teachers were called to the main hall, where Dr Ffurter had some news that seemed to upset him.

"I have just received word that the School Spectre is coming tomorrow," he told them all. "He's going to poke into every nook and cranny, assess your monstrous progress and write a report on us."

Dr Ffurter was so upset that he turned into a werewolf, jumped to the ground and howled at the moon that wasn't out yet.

"The Head's off his trolley," Lon said to Omar.

"He'll get back on it in a minute," Omar said. He was right. The werewolf jumped up onto the trolley and became the Head again.

"This school looks far too normal," the Head said. "We must tidy it down. Make it look disgraceful. I will order a fresh batch of skeletons and some more tarantulas and rats – *please* don't snack on the rats between meals, boys – and I expect every student to be on his worst behaviour while the Spectre is here."

"Can we spit in his eye?" one boy yelled out.

"I insist that you do," the Head replied. "If the Spectre thinks you aren't monstrous enough, he might close us down and send you to boring, normal schools, where they will teach you not to drop litter, cheek your elders, or fiddle with your bottoms in public. How would you like *that* then?"

Some of the boys groaned to show how little they would like it.

"So," the Head went on, "each class will be given a number of tasks, and I want you all to get to work at once and do your worst. This school must look and smell as foul as possible. Do I make myself clear?"

Lon and Omar went to their class with the rest of their year. Their class tutor was Professor Bloodless. "Your task, Year 7s," the Professor said, "is to go into the Wild and collect as many toads and slugs as you can to put in teachers' cups to make them sick. Boys who return empty-handed will be made to tuck their shirts in for a week. Off you go now!"

Grout, who was not a Year 7, had been listening outside the door. 'So,' he thought, 'these kids are going into the Wild, are they?' That gave him an idea. A plan for getting even with Lon for throwing his grandpa's hand to the school dog.

Chapter 6
Into the Wild

The Wild, as you might expect, was not a very welcoming place. The trees were tall and twisty, the rocks were rough and ready, and the stagnant streams were stinky.

The students were sent off in pairs, with lunch boxes and sacks. The sacks were for the toads and slugs they were to collect. But it wasn't just toads and slugs that lived in the Wild. Far from it. The Wild was full to bursting with monsters of every shape and kind. When some of the Year 7s came across these dreadful creatures, they found it very hard not to tremble and howl and run back to school shouting, "Mama!"

Lon and Omar met their fair share of monsters. They ran into red-eyed ogres, hungry for tasty boy meat. They hid from snarling hell-hounds and hissing wildcats. They ducked to avoid great birds with beaks like chainsaws and wings like garden spades. There were snakes with poisonous fangs, demons with dodgy horns, and headless horsemen on headless horses.

Think of any monster or horror you like, and it was there in the Wild.

But the two boys still managed to find 13 toads and 15 slugs, which they put into separate bags so the toads wouldn't eat the slugs, or the slugs cover the toads with slime.

Towards the middle of the afternoon, a heavy mist fell and most of the Year 7s returned to the school. Lon and Omar might have returned too, if they hadn't strayed too deep into the Wild and got lost. It was dangerous walking around out there when it was foggy, so Lon and Omar sheltered in a cave.

They lit a fire to keep warm and settled down to wait for the fog to lift. They wrapped their cloaks about them, and removed the strap-on bolts from their necks. They were much more comfortable without the bolts.

The fog did not lift. As misty afternoon gave way to misty night, Lon and Omar heard, imagined or felt all manner of spooky things – owls hooting, wings brushing their hair, creatures scuffling around them. Once they heard someone calling. They peered into the fog, and saw a dead shepherd calling his dead sheep home.

Around midnight, a bat appeared in the mouth of the cave. The bat grew in size and became a tall, thin man in a cape even blacker than the night.

"Are you a vampire?" Lon asked, trying to sound bold.

"I am," hissed the tall, thin man. "And I'm looking for blood. Shall I take yours, perhaps?"

"We'd rather you didn't," Omar said. "It helps keep us warm on a night like this."

"Aren't you afraid that I might take it, anyway?"

"Of course," Lon said. "But you have kind eyes, so I don't think you will."

The vampire was horrified. "Kind eyes? I've never been so insulted in my death! I wouldn't take your blood if it was the last drop on earth!" He turned back into a bat and flew away.

Chapter 7
Horror of Horrors

Lon and Omar must have fallen asleep at some point because they woke up at another. When they woke it was just after seven in the morning, but they had no way of knowing this. The fog had cleared enough for them to see four horrid creatures, with eyes as red as chilli peppers, lumbering towards the cave mouth.

These four creatures were as terrifying to behold as their moans were terrifying to hear.

Their faces looked like withered pumpkins and gave off a faint yellow glow. Their teeth were like pencil stubs. Their feet had six toes each, every one of them the size and colour of a bruised banana.

Lon gulped. "I feel a scream coming on," he said.

"That's nothing," said Omar. "I've just wet myself."

Lon and Omar were about to throw themselves into one another's arms when a rabbit hopped by the cave. It was a standard fluffy rabbit with a dear little tail and dear little ears. It was the kind of rabbit which, at any other time, the two boys would have liked to cuddle and stroke while saying "Aaaah" in soppy voices.

The four lumbering creatures did not seem to find the rabbit cuddly at all. When they saw it hop merrily by, they threw their arms in the air and shrieked like nobody's business. And as they shrieked dreadful things happened to them.

Their banana toes dropped off.

Their pencil-stub teeth fell out.

Their pumpkin heads fell apart.

It was then that Lon and Omar saw these monsters for what they really were. Four boys from Dr Ffurter's – Grout and his pals, Spook, Spittle and Clive. To Lon's surprise, the four boys lifted their bare feet, screamed and ran for it.

"You know, this time next year we'll be running from rabbits too," said Omar.

"We will?" said Lon. "Why?"

"When young monsters turn 12 they stop liking cuddly things, and start to fear them. Didn't you know that?"

"Ssh!" Lon said. "Quiet!"

He pointed to a fearsome beast dragging its monstrous shadow across the misty cave entrance. The two boys pressed back against the wall. Was this another practical joker, or a true beast of the Wild? But then the flickering light from their fire lit up the

monster's face and they knew that it was no joker.

"We have to get out of here," Lon whispered. "Quick, while he's looking the other way."

Omar had no idea why his friend was so afraid of this beast, but he didn't want to be left in the cave by himself. The boys grabbed their sacks of jumping toads and slithering slugs, sneaked out of the cave and ran for it.

As they ran, helter-skelter and willy-nilly, terrible creatures stepped out to try and catch them. Jaws opened to gobble them up. Bloodshot eyes rolled like bloody marbles. Mean claws reached for them. They escaped all of these horrors, but only just. They ran on and on and on without the faintest idea where they were going.

At last, they came to a high, old wall with a gap in it. They knew as well as you do that gaps in walls are meant to be climbed through – and through they went. And on the other side, they saw ...

"School!" Omar cried in relief.

A downstairs window was open and they clambered in, very glad indeed to be back. They started up the back stairs to their dorm. But ...

"Oh no!"

... they found their way blocked by Grout and his three pals – who did not look pleased to see them.

Chapter 8
The School Spectre

"Got lost then, did we?" Grout said. "Ah, poor diddums."

"At least we didn't run screaming from dear little bunny rabbits," Lon replied, but quietly.

"Hey, where are your bolts?" asked Spittle.

Lon and Omar clutched at their necks. They'd left their bolts in the cave!

"We took them out," Omar said. "You should try it some time. It's much more comfortable without them."

"You can't take your bolt out," said Spook. "Remove your bolt and your head falls off, everyone knows that. Once bolted, always bolted."

"It's not true," Lon said. "Try it – if you dare."

Grout, Spook, Spittle and Clive frowned at one another, not at all sure about this.

"What's up?" said Omar. "Scared?"

"Of course they are," Lon said. "Anyone who's scared of fluffy little bunnies would be scared of taking his bolt out. Some monsters!"

"Scared?" growled Grout. "I'll show you who's scared!"

He started struggling one-handed with his bolt. His three friends didn't want to seem scared either and so they followed his example. The bolts weren't easy to unscrew. They'd been in their necks for most of their lives and were only oiled on leap years.

"Need a hand?" Lon said to Grout, who was finding it even harder to get his bolt out than the others.

Grout went bright green with rage and yanked his bolt so hard with his single hand that it flew out. His pals managed to unscrew theirs at about the same time. Then the four stood grinning at one another.

"It's true," said Clive. "Unbolted heads don't fall off."

Grout sneered at Lon and Omar. "Scared, were we?"

But then, to the four boys' surprise (but not to Lon and Omar's), their heads tipped slowly forward, hit the floor and started bouncing down the stairs.

The four headless boys sat down in shock. "Help!" their heads wailed from the stairs below. "Put our bolts back!"

"I don't hear the magic word," Lon said.

"What magic word?" Grout's head said from the 5th step down.

"The one that starts with 'pl' and ends with 'ease'," Lon said.

"Please," the bouncing heads of Grout and the others begged. "Please, please, *please* put our bolts back!"

"What's in it for us?" said Omar.

"Put our bolts back and we won't play any more jokes on you or bully you ever again," said Grout's head.

"That doesn't sound much to me," Lon said. "Does it sound much to you, Omar?"

"No," said Omar. "Doesn't sound worth the bother to me."

"Wait," said Grout's head from the 9th step down. "We … we'll bring you breakfast in bed on trays every Sunday. How's that?"

Lon and Omar laughed with joy. "It's a deal!"

They went down and gathered up the four heads and bolted them back into place. They bolted Grout's head on the wrong way round until he complained.

"There is one thing I don't understand," Grout said when his head was on properly.

"Why don't your heads fall off? Only thing I can think of is that you're not real monsters."

"Careful," Lon said. "You have to be nice to us from now on."

"Grrr," said Grout. Being nice to these two was going to be the hardest thing he'd ever done.

Grout and his monstrous gang wandered away. They jerked their necks this way and that to make sure their heads were firmly fixed on.

Just at that minute, there was a mighty knock at the main door in the hall below. As usual, the door creaked open all by itself. Lon and Omar peered through the stair rails to see who the visitor was.

It was the terrifying creature they had run from at the cave!

"Tell the Head the School Spectre's here," the creature snapped at no one at all.

"Did you hear that?" Omar whispered. "He's the School Spectre!"

"I know," said Lon, as he crouched in the shadows.

"You know? Is that why you didn't want him to see you in the cave?"

"Sort of," Lon said.

Down in the hall, the Head's trolley zoomed into sight. "Delighted to see you again, Spectre!" he cried. "Care to join me in my study for a nice glass of warm blood before you tour the school? I have an excellent vintage, from the Dead Sea area. Or perhaps you would prefer a nice tumbler of chilled mucus?"

On the Head's orders, the school had been turned upside down and more horrors added everywhere. Bandaged mummies were propped up in corridors. Ghosts swung from broken chandeliers. Skeletons sat in old chairs. Dozens of extra cobwebs dangled from beams. Windows were cracked, doors were off their hinges, potted plants had been treated with rat poison, and so on.

"It's certainly an improvement on last time," the Spectre said, as the Head showed him round. "I hoped it would be. After all, I've just sent my own son here."

Lon and Omar's class of Year 7s, with the help of Professor Bloodless, had prepared a set of surprises for the Spectre. When he was shown into the classroom, a bucket of frogspawn fell on his head. Then he slipped on the floor, which they had greased with oil from a gorgon's armpit. Finally they took out their catapults and pelted him with paper pellets soaked in toilet water.

The Spectre dried his face with a cloth covered in soot, which one of the boys had handed him. "Top of the class, young monsters," he said. "I'm sure you'll do very well at Dr Ffurter's."

The Head winked at Professor Bloodless. All was well. The Spectre wouldn't close the school down after what he'd seen today.

Just as he was about to leave, the Spectre whispered something in the Head's ear. The Head called Lon out.

"They've noticed your bolts are missing," Grout hissed as Lon went by. "You're for it now."

Lon pulled his collar up and followed the School Spectre and the Head out of the room. In the corridor the Spectre asked Dr Ffurter to

leave them for a moment. Then he turned his dreadful gaze on Lon.

"Well, young monster, and how are you finding it?" he asked.

"Could be worse, I suppose," Lon answered.

"It's not easy being monstrous," the Spectre said. "You have to work at it."

"I know," said Lon.

The Spectre plunged his hand into his pocket and pulled out the two strap-on neck bolts that Lon and Omar had left in the cave. "I think these might belong to you," he said.

Lon fixed one of the strap-on bolts round his neck.

"When I next see you, Lon," the Spectre said sternly, "I expect you to be much nastier and uglier than this. I want to be scared out of my wits by you. Is that understood?"

Lon sighed. He had quite a task ahead of him. It wasn't going to be easy, but he had no choice.

"I'll do my best, Father," he said. "Promise."

Our books are tested
for children and young people by
children and young people.

Thanks to everyone who consulted on
a manuscript for their time and effort in
helping us to make our books better
for our readers.